RIN(

A NATIONAL RITE OF PASSAGE:
For the New and Promised Generation

Estella Conwill Majozo

RINGSHOUT!
A NATIONAL RITE OF PASSAGE:
For the New and Promised Generation

ISBN: 1-59232-266-2

Printed in the United States of America

Contents

Dedication

To the King of Ages and the Author of Life

And for my grandchildren: James Elijah Lowe, Dominic Landen Alexander, Noah Justice Alexander, Avery Jonae Alexander, and the entire new and promised generation

This gift is presented to:

____

By:

____

Date:

____

Your signature (agreement to make this rite of passage):

____

Your partner's signature (agreement to assist):

____

Acknowledgments

With gratitude beyond words, I thank the following people:

Dr. Houston Conwill, sculptor, public art collaborator
Dr. William L. Conwill, Harrison-Conwill Associates, consultant/facilitator
Dr. Patrice Lowe and Jim Lowe, Lowe Learning System, consultants/facilitators
SSG Dominic Alexander and Tashara Alexander
Spivey Conwill and Kinshasha Holman Conwill

Dr. Yalonda JD Green, actor/facilitator; Alphonso Green, actor
Dr. William Hamilton Jr., actor/facilitator; William Hamilton III, actor
Dr. David Anderson, actor/facilitator; Marion Smith, actor
Antonio Losavio, actor; Tanya Robertson, facilitator; Todd Green, vocalist
Karen Edwards-Hunter, director; Earbie Johnson, percussionist
Ed Chestnut and Company, recording musicians

Donald Woolridge, Kappa Alpha Psi Fraternity, Inc., Achievement Award; Tommy and Gloria Morrow, Inland Valley News, Creativity in Arts Award; The Pleiades Theatre Company, Salute to Seven Sisters Pleiades Star Award; Supergirls, Inc., Superwoman Award!
Papa Aly Ndaw, Femmes Africa Solidarite Conference, Bamako, Mali/Africa
Dr. J. Blaine Hudson, The National Black Family Conference
The Juneteenth Theatre Festival; University of Louisville
Xavier University, New Orleans, Louisiana
Mary Katherine Harris, Los Angeles, California
Dr. Judylyn S. Ryan, Ohio Wesleyan University
Dr. Robert L. Douglas, artist (genealogy exhibition)
Cheri Bryant Hamilton, Louisville Metro Council
Mary Jefferson, Dream Keepers, Inc.
Dr. Shanna Smith, graduate assistant
Shauna Taylor Evans, personal assistant

The Pilgrimage Site/The African Burial Ground

The public art team of sculptor Houston Conwill, architect Joseph DePace, and poet Estella Conwill Majozo created the **New Ringshout Cosmogram.** It is a commissioned, forty-foot monument commemorating the African Burial Ground in New York City. The cosmogram inspired the writing of this rite of passage and memorializes many of the ancestral voices celebrated here. The ground itself is hailed as the most important archaeological find of the twentieth century and was named a National Monument. The GSA's African Burial Ground Project (which includes the outdoor monument by Rodney Leon, the indoor New Ringshout Cosmogram, and several other art works, research, and rituals) was recognized by the White House with a *Preserve America Presidential Award.*

Everyone who completes *Ringshout! A National Rite of Passage* is encouraged to visit the African Burial Ground as our designated pilgrimage site at least once during your lifetime.

Introduction

Estella Conwill Majozo's *Ringshout! A National Rite of Passage: For the New and Promised Generation* presents new possibilities for healing our young people as they face the obstacles they find on their path to maturity as Black man and women. These obstacles include living in a society that diminishes their humanity, distorts their level of awareness, presents them with contradictory messages about themselves, infantilizes and sexualizes them, and encourages them to live in fear and hate. These are formidable impediments to healthy personal, interpersonal, community, and social development. Majozo encodes the map for overcoming these obstacles in the word *Xenia,* the antithesis of xenophobia.

Despite the post-racial rhetoric of Black resilience in the wake of Barack Obama's election as President of the United States, many of our young people have lost track of healthy paths to our Black cultural wellsprings and touchstones. Many point to historical events—the forced migration from the African continent, alternatively known as the Middle Passage, the Maafa, or the holocaust of enslavement; centuries of living in bondage; and generations living under The Black Codes designed to maintain subservience and economic dependence—as causal.

Xenia provides a map for the new generation as they join in the Ringshout: knowing their people, recognizing who/whose they are, positioning themselves strategically on the path, staying on course, and living fearlessly with love.

William L. Conwill, Ph.D.

But you are a chosen generation, a royal priesthood, a holy nation, a peculiar people; that you should show forth the praises of him who hath called you out of darkness into his marvelous light.

1 Peter 2:9 (NKJV)

Please read the fifty segments in sequence and with your partner. Ready? Begin.

1

The Ten Passages of Endurance

Say the following aloud with your partner! (Your partner reads the first line and you follow with the italicized words, and so on.)

Through our captivity into slavery!
Our God has sustained us!

Through the horrendous Middle Passage!
Our God has sustained us!

Through the degradation of the auction block!
Our God has sustained us!

Through the years of merciless labor!
Our God has sustained us!

Through our great emancipation!
Our God has sustained us!

Through the brutality of Jim Crow!
Our God has sustained us!

Through our relentless protest against injustice!
Our God has sustained us!

Through our attainment of civil rights!
Our God has sustained us!

Through our struggle toward full integration!
Our God has sustained us!

Through the attainment of the presidency of the United States of America!
Our God has sustained us! Our God has sustained us!
With gratitude we acknowledge, our God has sustained us!

2

The Five Xenia Challenges: Become an Indomitable Hero

Ringshout! A National Rite of Passage is a tale of our great and powerful people who were called by almighty God to survive the horrors of slavery and resist some of the most brutal oppression inflicted upon mankind in the past five hundred years.

It is an ongoing, interactive tale that functions as a rite of passage and features you, a member of the new and promised generation, as the main character and, as you step into your sacred purpose, an indomitable hero. Across race, ethnicity, class, and gender, you are invited to make this rite of passage and become a more enlightened, compassionate, mature, and spiritually empowered human being.

The initiation has five challenges. They are all coded in a little five-letter word, *xenia,* which means hospitality (the opposite of xenophobia), taking on the other, and, in its highest expression, love. It's being at home in your own cultural skin and not being afraid to let others in.

Say the five challenges aloud.

XENIA

X—X-Ray the Soul
E—Exalt Those Worthy of Praise
N—Negotiate
I—Interrogate
A—Adapt for a Brand-New Phase

The First Xenia Challenge

X

X-Ray!

X-Ray the Soul: The Five and the Ten

Where there is no vision, the people perish.
Proverbs 29:18

3

The Three Shinings: Marked Periods of Grace

When you look through history at the soul of our people, what you'll see is the *five* and the *ten*. This pattern goes beyond the fact that ten million of our African ancestors survived the Middle Passage (the largest forced migration in world history) and that one-fifth of the original number now make up the bridge of bones lining the ocean's bottom.

Whenever these two numbers or the leaders marked by these two numbers, rise up at the same historical moment, their rising and crossing create what is called a *shining*. The two leaders in a shining usually pronounce their identity as the Five or the Ten in a very public manner.

Unlike an eclipse, where one star blocks another body's light, the crossing in a shining intensifies the light of the two leaders, marking periods of special grace.

Our history has three major shinings:

1. Mr. Booker T. Washington and Dr. W.E.B. Dubois.
2. Mr. Malcolm X and Dr. Martin Luther King Jr.
3. This historical moment with two important people from our history that you will identify.

4

Cultural Prophets from the Male Genealogy

The First Shining: Booker T. Washington and W.E.B. DuBois

At the first shining, Booker T. Washington in his most famous speech at the Atlanta World Exposition said, "In all things that are purely social we can be as separate as the [five] fingers, yet one as the hand in all things essential to mutual progress!" He said more that day, but the "five fingers" marked him.

His counterpart, W.E.B. DuBois, a founding father of the NAACP, projected his hope for the race through "The Talented Tenth"—that most gifted among us who would inspire others to achievement.

The Second Shining: Malcolm X and Martin Luther King Jr.

In the second shining, Malcolm Little became Malcolm X. The *X* represented his unknown African name. However, it also is the Roman numeral ten.

Unlike Malcolm X who sought justice by any means necessary Martin Luther King Jr.'s nonviolent way of confronting injustice—even in the face of bullets, bombs, and bloodhounds—was fixed on the fifth commandment, "Thou shalt not kill."

Malcolm X took on nine names in his quest for true identity and was eulogized in his tenth manifestation as "Our Shining Prince."

King had always been King. But he got his proper naming a generation before when his father went to Germany with ten other ministers and was so impressed with Martin Luther's Reformation that he renamed himself and his son. (Martin was originally Michael.)

On the day before Dr. King was assassinated, he declared with the brilliance of a shining Moses, "I may not get there with you, but

I want you to know tonight, that we as a people will get to the Promised Land!"

These fathers in our male genealogy (Washington and DuBois as well as Malcolm and Dr. King) may have appeared to be bitter enemies, but in fact they were twins—cultural prophets whose rising and crossing created light.

5

Fives and Tens All over the Place (A Collabo Rap!)

Rap this with your partner! (Your partner says the first two lines and you follow with the italicized words, and so on.)

Come on! Light! Light! Diffusion and grace!
With fives and tens
all over the place!

The sit-ins at Woolworth's,
a five-and-dime store!
King's birthday, the tenth holiday—
but wait, there's more.

The Montgomery Bus Boycott,
the day Rosa Parks arrived,
December holy fifth,
nineteen fifty-five!

And the Buffalo soldiers,
they never turned back!
The Tenth Calvary Regiment
of the US Army, Jack!

And the Million Man March,
Minister Farrakhan was no jive!
He said, "I stand before you with an eight-point plan,
of which atonement is number five!"

And what's the first word of Dr. King's
"I Have a Dream" speech?
"Five score years ago—"
Go on now, teach!

"A great American," Abraham Lincoln!
"in whose symbolic shadow we stand

signed the Emancipation Proclamation.
Now you're starting to understand.

Now there's just one more from our history
that we've got to revive.
Turn to the person next to you and say,
come on—give me five!

That's old school for dap.
It ain't rap, but it's live!
You know what I'm saying—
give it up, give me five!

However you checking it,
Ebonic-ly perfecting it,
I'm through with dissecting it,
so come on, give me five*!*

[The X-ray soul challenge! The third shining!]
Now it's time for the third shining. Here's a little hint:
The five in the third shining is the first Black president!
President Barack Obama! Yes, but how do you know?
Just because he has five letters in his name? *No!*

Just because he's conscious? If that's what it takes,
make it Jessie Jackson, rapper Fifty Cent, or DMX, for heaven's sakes!
What did Obama say in the campaign that marked the man?
"*There are five things America can do to begin to lead again.*"

Okay, he's the five. Now, close your eyes for the ten.
This is a person who never gives in.
He's got the philosophical impulse of a W.E.B.
and the cooperative economic spirit of a Booker T.

He's got King's sense of justice, Malcolm's search for the real.
His example will touch hundreds in the ripple appeal.

You know this person, young people. Just look within.
Okay, now who is it? *I am the ten!*

6

I'm the Number Ten

Rap the following and mean it!

I'm the tenth generation up from slavery.
I'm the number ten—number ten, that's me!

Generation X with a whole new spin.
Bottom line is, I'm called to win!

I'm a culture-bearer from a long, long line.
Unstoppable force—I'm sent to *shine!*

Dignity's banging beneath my skin.
I know who I am—I'm the number ten!

(Write) I am the ten! ______________________________

7

The Spiritual Blueprint: X-Ray the Soul

Now take it deeper. Look at the spiritual blueprint.

Each of the five challenges reflects a different sacred mystery that connects us with the divine. In a word, God has His own shining—His own sacred *five* and *ten:*

The Ten Commandments tell us how to live,

And the *five* wounds of Jesus make it possible for us to do so.

Say the Ten Commandments aloud:

1. I am the Lord, your God, you shall not have strange gods before me.
2. You shall not take the name of the Lord God in vain.
3. Remember to keep holy the Lord's Day.
4. Honor your father and your mother.
5. You shall not kill.
6. You shall not commit adultery.
7. You shall not steal.
8. You shall not bear false witness.
9. You shall not covet your neighbor's wife.
10. You shall not covet your neighbor's goods.

Deuteronomy 5:6–21

8

A Declaration of Identity: I Am a Child of God

Let this sacred shining and our alignment with it remind you that God is not a respecter of persons. He loves and has great compassion for all people—even those who are deemed by others as being "among the least of these." Our ancestors sang it this way in one of the spirituals:

> If anybody asks you who I am—who I am—who I am
> If anybody asks you who I am—
> Tell 'em I'm a child of God!

This song flies in the face of the stereotypical, counterfeit labels constantly bombarding your mind. Indeed, you are not the N-word! Your identity is not summed up in the abusive B-word! You are not a gangsta, thug, or loser! These terms demean and denigrate your true nature. Stop a moment and renew your mind. You are who God says you are.

Say and write these five affirmations. (Your partner says the italicized words.)

I am a child of God! ______________________________
John 1:12 (NKJV) says: "But as many as received Him, to them He gave the right to become children of God, even to them who believe in his name."

I am the head and not the tail! ______________________________
Deuteronomy 28:13 (NKJV) says: "The Lord will make you the head and not the tail."

I am the righteousness of God! ______________________________
2 Corinthians 5:21 (NKJV) says: "God made the one who did not know sin to be sin for us, so that in him we would become the righteousness of God."

I am the temple of the Holy Spirit! ______________________
Corinthians 6:19 (NKJV) says: "Or do you not know that your body is a temple of the Holy Spirit who is in you, whom you have from God, and you are not your own?"

I am more than a conqueror! ___________________________
Romans 8:37 (NKJV) says: "Yet in all these things we are more than conquerors through Him Who loved us."

9

All Souls Face Adversity: "A Web of Mutuality"

Say this with your partner! (Your partner says the first three lines and you follow with the italicized words, and so on.)

All souls face adversity.
Look through the ages, what do you see?
Blacks endured the Middle Passage years—
Native Americans, the Trail of Tears.

We labored mercilessly in the fields,
the Chinese in factories with little yield.
The Black man was defined as three-fifths of a man.
The Irish were treated cruelly throughout the land.

We struggled against the Jim Crow bar,
Japanese-Americans in camps like Manzanar.
We were lynched and tarred with no one to tell.
The Klan hated the Jewish people as well.

We're racially profiled everyday that's sent,
since 9/11, it's Americans of Arab descent,
and Mexican-Americans, too,
who have bled for the red, white, and blue.

When we remember martyrs, Medgar Evers and King,
the names, Chaney, Goodman, and Schwerner also ring.
When we remember the four little girls and Emmitt Till,
the spirits of John and Robert Kennedy will not keep still.

It's a complicated tale—can't you see?
King says "We're caught in a web of mutuality."
Inescapably bound—you and me.
The struggle continues till all are free!
The struggle continues till all are free!

10

Mirroring Warriors: On Both Sides of the Color Line

Our condition during slavery was inhumane and included such atrocities as these ten: dispossession of self; brutal beatings with whips; bonding with chains; branding with flesh-burning irons; auctioning of our naked bodies; the mounting of heavy, bridle-head pieces; the dismembering of body parts; the separation of families; vicious rapes; and murders.

And yet, individuals rose up and defied the injustice. The quest for freedom has always had mirroring warriors on both sides of the color line. Some of them included these brave souls.

Frederick Douglass published the newspaper, The *North Star* to expose the evils of slavery!	**William Lloyd Garrison** edited *The Liberator* to support the abolitionist cause!
Nat Turner led a revolt against slavery on southern plantations.	**John Brown** staged an insurrection at Harpers Ferry.
Thousands of African Americans shed their blood in the Civil War.	**President Abraham Lincoln** signed the Emancipation Proclamation and lost his life at the hand of an assassin.
Washington and DuBois dedicated their lives to uplifting the race.	**William Wilberforce** helped build Wilberforce University, the first college owned and operated by African Americans.
Dr. Martin Luther King Jr. led the March on Washington for equal rights.	**President Lyndon B. Johnson** was at the US Capitol to sign the 1963 Civil Rights Act into law.
Barack Obama took the presidential oath.	**Joseph Biden** became his vice president in a supportive, nonpaternalistic manner.

President Abraham Lincoln said this regarding his stance: "Sir, my concern is not whether God is on our side; my greatest concern is to be on God's side, for God is always right."

President Barack Obama imparted his vision this way: "We cannot help but believe that the old hatreds shall someday pass; that the lines of the tribe shall soon dissolve; that as the world grows smaller, our common humanity shall reveal itself."

Whatever you become, your real challenge is to recognize, respect, and renew the diminished humanity in yourself and others. Your challenge, Young Initiate, is to *shine.*

This is your time! Pay attention to the Five and the Ten!

George Zimmerman's murder of seventeen-year-old Trayvon Martin is part of a larger continuum in our striving for truth and justice. Trayvon's death during your lifetime, like that of Emmit Till during the Civil Rights era, raised our awareness of the tensions surrounding issues of race and quality.

Trayvon's tens are unmistakable. He was on a ten-day suspension from school. Besides Skittles and iced tea, he had in his possession ten cents. For ten days only the Florida media covered the story, and within weeks, *hoodie marches* were held in ten major cities.

Five days after the not-guilty verdict, President Obama made his Xenia pronouncement. He fully identified with the other by saying, "You know, when Trayvon Martin was first shot, I said that this could have been my son. Another way of saying that is Trayvon Martin could have been me, thirty-five years ago." He asked Americans to "do some soul searching" in the aftermath of the shooting death of the unarmed, Black teenager.

In this third shining, you will have numerous opportunities to do your own soul searching. This is your time. This is your turn as a member of a people chosen for God's own possession to change the world.

Take to heart the words of Coretta Scott King, Dr. Martin Luther King's wife: "Freedom is never really won. You earn it and win it in every generation."

Remember that regardless of your race, ethnicity, gender, or class, and which profession you hold (teacher, lawyer, elected official, first responder, activist, healer, athlete, artist, and so on), you are first and foremost a guardian, a bearer of God's transformative light. Your calling is to be a child of God and live in the truth that makes us free.

As a conclusion of the first challenge, rap again, "I'm the Number Ten."

I'm the tenth generation up from slavery.
I'm the number ten—number Ten, that's me!

Generation X with a whole new spin.
Bottom line is I'm called to win.

I'm a culture-bearer from a long, long line.
Unstoppable force, I'm sent to shine.

Dignity's banging beneath my skin.
I know who I am—I'm the number Ten!

Review

Remember these terms. Begin consciously to speak the language of freedom.

- ✓ Xenia
- ✓ Middle Passage—The Maafa
- ✓ The Emancipation Proclamation
- ✓ Jim Crow
- ✓ Freedom
- ✓ Shining—The Five and the Ten
- ✓ Mutuality
- ✓ Integrity
- ✓ Grace
- ✓ The Ten Commandments

You learned there are Ten Passages of Endurance and Five Ringshout Challenges. You also discovered the acronym, XENIA (a five-letter word that begins with an *X*)! You learned there are three shinings that together feature Five prominent figures from our male genealogy—Washington, DuBois, Malcolm, Dr. King, and Obama! You learned that you are the number Ten of the Third Shining! You learned there is one Sacred Shining that consists of the Ten Commandments and the Five Wounds of our crucified Savior.

Write the most important lesson you learned while X-raying the soul!

____

____

Think of other Fives and Tens. The Jackson Five, the Black Codes (one of which forbad African Americans from gathering in groups of more than five), the Black Panther Party's ten-point plan, the tenth letter of the alphabet, *J*, for Jesus! You can remember so much history through this Shining pattern. Share one more. How about *fiveology*—the spoken word poetry collective!

____

The Second Xenia Challenge

E

Exalt!

Exalt Those Worthy of Praise:
The Female Genealogy

Oh Lord, our Lord, how excellent is your name in all the earth!
Psalm 8:1 (NKJV)

11

A Message in the Ancestral Names

In the movie, *Roots* by Alex Haley, Kunta Kinte repeatedly resisted being called Toby by his enslaver. "Kunta Kinte!" he insisted at each lash of the whip, and that name pronounced by a griot (an oral historian) sealed Haley's ten-year search for his African roots.

Haley sat in the circle of elders beneath the simmering African sun listening for hours to the griot pronounce decades of memorized history before he finally heard the report that corroborated the tale that he had heard all his life. In the village of Juffure, a boy named Kunta Kinte had been out gathering wood to make a drum for his rite of passage when he was captured by the tubob. Remarkable! This identical tale had been passed down to Haley through seven generations, and it was grounded in a name. He was, indeed, the great, great, great, great grandson of Kunta Kinte.

In Maya Angelou's *I Know Why the Caged Bird Sings*, Mrs. Cullens (the woman she works for) insists on calling her Mary because Margaret is too long. After Maya breaks her heirloom china and bolts from her house, the woman concedes to her friend, "Her name is Margaret!"

The Historical Ringshout!

Like Kinte's and Angelou's insistence, the historical Ringshout is the community's effort to self-define. In that ritual, our ancestors danced in a circle and called out the names of the nations from which they were severed. At a time when family names had been stripped from them and they were treated as chattel and given names of their enslavers (for example, Jefferson, Washington, Jackson), the chanting helped them reclaim their identity and dignity.

The nations below are the same ones in the New Ringshout, a monument commemorating the African Burial Ground in New York City. (See the end of this book.)

We are Fulani!
We are Fon!
We are Wolof!
And Kono!—
Ashanti! Akan!
Mende! And Edo!

We are Idoma! Yoruba!
Batawa! Ga!
Twi! Itsekir!
Tikar! And Lodagaa!

We are Kpelle!
And Nupe!
And Tiv! And Hausa!
Igbo! Bamun!
Ewe! And Igbira!

In our New Ringshout Chant, we not only recall the names of the nations in the motherland. We exalt the names of the mothers themselves. Indeed, the words of Alice Walker ring true: "How simple a thing it seems to me that to know ourselves as we are, we must know our mothers' names."

The chant you are about to see consists of the first syllable of the first name of eight powerful Black women who have helped sustain us from the time of our enslavement to the present generation. In a pattern no less than mystical, the syllables put together, as they appear chronologically, make a statement. In other words, the first syllable of each woman's first name together says something very important. After you decode the message, you will see that our very survival has been inscribed in the names of our mothers.

This is interesting because several of them had names changes to the ones we see in this message. One of the mothers was enslaved as a child and brought to America—she surely must have had a different name in Africa. Another received her name from God because she would be travelling the land and telling His truth to the people. Still another was originally called Araminta Ross. The final name changes and their compilation support the ancestral saying, "God writes straight on crooked lines!"

12

The New Ringshout Chant

The New Ringshout Chant is in Black Vernacular English, or Ebonics, a speech developed after our African languages were stripped from us during enslavement.

You might recognize your grandmother's tongue—the dialect she uses when giving advice that must be heeded—or the tone of your great uncle when he lifts the newborn at the family reunion.

It's the voice you dream in—the one that rises from the preacher's lips when he's telling about a God who makes a way out of no way. It's the language that keeps on changing like the hip-hop of artists, Common and Beyoncé on the radio—their old school samplings overlaying our unerasable lives.

Chant and listen for the first syllable of the first names. Feel free to improvise!

Fi So Ha / I Be / Ma Jo Zo!
Fi So Ha / I Be / Ma Jo Zo!
Fi So Ha / I Be /Ma Jo Zo!
Fi So Ha / I Be/ Ma Jo Zo!

13

A Threefold Challenge

Your challenge is threefold:

> One: Identify the full names of the mothers.
>
> Two: Put the syllables together and decode the message.
>
> Three: Find some creative way to give the information back to show you truly grasp the meaning.

You must give the names in one hundred five seconds! That's one second for each day our ancestors spent in the Middle Passage, also known as the African Diaspora holocaust, or the Maafa.

14

Identity the Full Names: The Female Genealogy

Identify the full names. Have your partner time you. You get one hundred five seconds. Write the names in the blanks after the syllables.

Fi ______________________________

The first African American woman to publish a book of poems. She had a different name before coming to America at age seven.

Phyllis Wheatley!

So ______________________________

A women's rights activist. Her birth name was Isabella Baumfree. She is best known for the speech: "Ain't I a Woman?"

Sojourner Truth!

Ha ______________________________

Conductor of the Underground Railroad. Moses! Originally named Araminta Ross. She boasted, "I never lost a passenger! And I never ran the train off track."

Harriet Tubman

I ______________________________

A journalist who brought lynching into the international spotlight. She wrote, "The nineteenth century lynching mob cuts off ears, toes, and fingers, strips of flesh and distributes portions of the body as souvenirs among the crowd."

Ida B. Wells

Be ______________________________

Empress of the blues. She once said, "I ain't good looking, but I'm somebody's angel child!"

Bessie Smith (Three more to go!)

Ma ______________________________

She founded the Black girls' college, was a member of Roosevelt's Black cabinet, and said: "Next to God, we are indebted to women, first for life itself, and then for making it worth living."

Mary McLeod Bethune

Jo ______________________________

Dancer extraordinaire! The darling of France! Mother of twelve adopted children—The Rainbow Tribe. She said, "Since I personified the savage on stage, I tried to be as civilized as possible in daily life."

Josephine Baker

Zo ______________________________

Harlem Renaissance writer/anthropologist. She presented authentic images of our life. She said, "Momma exhorted her children at every opportunity to 'jump at the sun!'"

Zora Neale Hurston

15

Decode the Message

The spirituals carried coded messages for the Underground Railroad. "Steal away to Jesus" was about more than religious ecstasy. It was about running away. "Wade in the Water" was about more than baptism. The runaways doused themselves in the rivers so bloodhounds wouldn't pick up their scent.

The dances performed by our ancestors carried subversive messages as well. This is true throughout the Diaspora. In America, they danced the Cakewalk, openly mocking the arrogant mannerisms of the enslaver. In Trinidad, they danced the Limbo, bending with incredible dexterity from the imagined nave of the ship and then assuming the posture for escape. In the Dominican Republic, they moved to the rhythms of the Merengue; chained in sugar fields, they stepped in unison to slip away.

The New Ringshout Chant in line with this tradition carries a message that initiates can share for years to come. To meet the second part of the Challenge, put the syllables together and decipher that message

Fi So Ha / I Be/ Ma Jo Zo

Write the message: ______________________________

Feel so high I be majo (a wonder-working) soul!

Now chant the message and let it inspire your spirit!

Feel so high I be majo soul!

16

A Creative Response: Give It All Back

Now we come to the third part of the challenge: Give it all back. The three Shinings, the *five* and the *ten,* the mothers' names, the diffusion, and the Xenia love.

Your response should be a signifying rap hook or a short poem. Remember, you're endowed with the impulse to survive, create, and grow.

Write your creative response!

17

The Ringshout Rap: (A Collabo Rap!)

Rap this with your partner! (You say the italicized words.)

So glad I know ancestors' names!

Why don't you take it on out—

I'm gonna shine the flame!
Flying high, see,
in righteous harmony
decoding destiny.

Ah you doing it, G!

There ain't no contradiction,
just the pure as light conviction
that this life, it ain't no fiction.

Let it roll, see!

The living scroll's the key!

Martin and Malcolm!
DuBois and Booker T.!

The million plus the ten
coming strong with me!

Wonder-working soul! Majo, free!

Bright begetting bright.

Say you want to be free!
Ringshout the route
Round about
Take it out!

I say Fi-So Ha!
I be Majo Zo!

Checking sweet Harriet
swinging down low.

Ida be rapping

Truth, don't blow!
Ten generations
catch the light in your eyes.
Dig the diffusion till you recognize
Love—it takes courage.
Don't you go for the lies!

Fi So Ha—

Pass it on—yo yo

Majo the meaning—
Respect your culture—

There you go.

Remember where you came from!

Peace out!

Be the glow!

Remember where you came from!
Peace out! Be the glow!

18

Disclosures: Keep It Real

Sometimes our flaws were as blatant as a black eye. Frederick Douglass's first attempt to escape slavery was ruined by betrayal. Malcolm was murdered by one of our own. And every time we celebrate Dr. King's birthday, somebody is there to remind us of his frailties. And the black-on-black crime in our communities certainly denies our stature. But for the record, despite our deficiencies, you should know this as well.

We are people made in God's image. The ones He drew from the waters of the Middle Passage, and through the fires of the Civil War and the ravages of Jim Crow. By His grace we built families, churches, schools, and communities in a place where it was once illegal to own ourselves, to claim each other as family, or to read.

In the midst of oppression, God gave us new and witty inventions that changed the fate of nations—Eli Whitney's cotton gin that sparked the Industrial Revolution; Lewis Latimer's carbon filament that made the light bulb assessable to everyone; Charles Drew's preservation of blood plasma that continues to save the lives of millions; Patricia Bath's Laserphaco Probe for the removal of cataracts; Garret Morgan's gas mask that spared soldiers of World War I from chemical warfare. All were life-enhancing, not destructive, inventions.

We gave birth to the blues, the spirituals, jazz, and gospel. We created art so visionary it makes you see the future. Our dances are imitated around the world!

We've proven ourselves as champions in the ring, conquerors on the court, and defeaters on the field. We've become civic leaders, ambassadors, and Nobel laureates! Rising from the lowest rung of oppression, we are both litmus and catalyst in this democracy.

The chant of our mothers' names reverberates the African proverb: "I am because we are; and because we are, therefore I am!" Indeed, we are here because they were there surviving, hoping, dreaming, working, and making a way out of no way!'

If you ever have an impulse to cheat yourself, sell out, or dishonor your legacy, stop and remember who you are: You are the number Ten, called through the names of the ancestors to be a wonder-working soul!

The following women warriors were on both sides of the color line.

Sojourner Truth delivered important speeches as an abolitionist and women's rights advocate.	**Harriet Beecher Stowe** published the provocative book, *Uncle Tom's Cabin*!
Mary McLeod Bethune fought for the education of young girls and founded Bethune Cookman College.	**First Lady Eleanor Roosevelt** advocated for the Tuskegee Airmen's service as active fighter pilots.
Ida B. Wells published *The Red Record* on the atrocities of lynching and brought the plight to the attention of the international community.	**Jessie Daniels Ames** founded The Association of Southern Women for the Prevention of Lynching, challenging the notion that white women needed protection from African American men.
Josephine Baker aided the French Resistance during World War II by smuggling information written in invisible ink on her sheet music.	**Ann Braden,** civil rights activist, was ostracized as communist in her efforts to achieve justice.
Zora Neale Hurston wrote authentic, classical portrayals of Black life.	**Helen Keller** wrote and supported equal rights for women and Blacks.

Turn to your partner and say aloud: "At our best, we are wonder-working souls!"

19

The Spiritual Blueprint: Exalt!

The names of the mothers can ward off weariness, but the name of Jesus wards off death!

Philippians 2:9 (NKJV) says, "Wherefore God hath highly exalted him, and given him a name which is above every name; that at the name of Jesus every knee should bow, of things in heaven, and things in earth, and things under the earth; And that every tongue should confess that Jesus Christ is Lord, to the glory of God the Father."

Furthermore, Romans 10:9 (NKJV) says, "If you confess with your mouth 'Jesus is Lord,' and believe in your heart that God raised Him from the dead, you will be saved."

Simply and sincerely confess with your mouth and believe in your heart.

20

How Majestic Is Your Name

Say this poem and let God encircle you.

Abba.
Father.
The Great I Am!

Comforter.
Deliverer.
Holy Lamb.

Immanuel.
Jehovah.
Lord of hosts!

Wonderful.
Counselor.
Holy Ghost!

Unspeakable Gift.
Only Begotten Son.
Quickening Spirit.
Resurrection.

God!
The Way!
The Truth!
The Life!

Yahweh!
Jesus!
Bread of Life.

21

A New Ringshout Name

This is the message we have heard from Him and declare to you: God is light; in Him there is no darkness at all. If we claim to have fellowship with Him yet walk in darkness, we lie and do not live by the truth. But if we walk in light, as He is in the light, we have fellowship with one another, and the blood of Jesus, his Son, purifies us from all sin.

1 John 1:5

We sometimes take the name of the one whose life we defend. During South Africa's Apartheid, many declared, "I am Mandela!" More recently, many wore T-shirts that said, "I am Trayvon!" Some who completed this rite of passage also took names. Call me Majozo! (*Ma*ry McLeod Bethune, *Jo*sephine Baker, and *Zo*ra Neale Hurston!) Call me Makiwadu! (*Ma*lcolm X, Martin Luther *Ki*ng Jr., Booker T. *Wa*shington, and W.E.B. *Du*Bois!)

You might want to take a Xenia name to add to your birth name. I urge you to take this decision seriously. Think of your role models, the people you admire, who you are, and want to become. Pray about it and then decide.

If you choose to take a name, you might want to creatively construct it. Duma! (*Dou*glass and *Ma*lcolm!) Sofi! (*So*journer Truth and *Phy*llis Wheatley!) Waki! (*Wa*shington and *Ki*ng!) Or even Ibe! (*I*da Wells and *Be*ssie Smith—"I be anything I want to be!")

Should you choose a Xenia name, write it here: ____________________

Above all, own that you are a child of God! That is your truest identity! Your sir name, Young Initiate, is Christ!

Review

Remember these terms. Make the language of liberation part of your discourse and self-determination.

- ✓ Ringshout
- ✓ African Diaspora
- ✓ Black Vernacular English—Ebonics
- ✓ Underground Railroad
- ✓ The Rainbow Tribe
- ✓ Harlem Renaissance
- ✓ Diffusion
- ✓ Tuskegee Airmen
- ✓ The Red Record
- ✓ Makiwadu

You learned that the first syllable of the first name of our mothers carries an important message: "Feel So High I Be MaJo Soul!" This statement is declarative and imperative. You learned that chanting the names and remembering the achievements of the mothers can ward off weariness. You learned that taking on the name of Jesus can ward off death.

What lesson did you learn while exalting those worthy of praise? Write it here:

____

____

You could easily include other names among the celebrated eight, including *Be*tty Shabazz! (Malcolm X's wife); *B*essie Coleman (first African-American female pilot); and *Ma*dame C.J. Walker (the first self-made millionaire). Not to mention those whose names would never fit the pattern, for instance, Queen Mother Moore (the founder of the Committee for Reparations for Descendants of US slaves). These eight women in the chant are emblematic of millions.

Name two others whose name resonate with those in the Ringshout Chant.

____

____

The Third Xenia Challenge

N

Negotiate!

Negotiate Strategies toward Attaining Your Goal: The Eight Steps of the New Ringshout Dance

Direct my steps by Your word, And let not iniquity have dominion over me.

Psalm 119:133 (NKJV)

22

The New Ringshout Dance: Strategies of Survival

Most countries have a dance that tells the story of their people's achievements. We do, too. And quiet as it's kept, it's not the Moonwalk! In the New Ringshout Dance, the women in the Chant are partners to eight extraordinary men. And the New Ringshout Dance is basically eight political positions taken by those ancestral couples that continue to inspire us today. It's a telling, beautiful, disciplined dance.

Your challenge—should you choose to accept it—is to perform the dance.

Like the women paired with them, the men in the dance are serious warriors. They include a leader in the antislavery movement (Frederick Douglass); the founder of the Back-to-Africa Movement (Marcus Garvey); a journalist who used the privilege of his light complexion to pass as white and infiltrate the Ku Klux Klan to expose their evil (Walter White); a world-class athlete who could "float like a butterfly and sting like a bee!" (Muhammad Ali); and a timeless renaissance poet who "bathed in the Euphrates when dawns were young" (Langston Hughes). Like the partnering women, they are royalty in our eyes!

As the main character of the Ringshout's unfolding tale, you should know that the dance not only empowers you. It can expose your weakness as well.

23

Choreography: The Dance that Tells the Story

Learn the craft of knowing how to open your heart and to turn on your creativity.

Judith Jamaison

I believe that dance came from the people and that it should always be delivered back to the people.

Alvin Ailey

Perform the following dance as your partner reads the choreography!

First Step—Phyllis Wheatley and Joseph Cinque!
Your palms before you—the slave ship, okay?

Second Step—hands to the sky!
Sojourner Truth and Douglass speak against the lie!

Third Step—running! That's right, hold.
Garvey's "Back to Africa!" Harriet's Road!

Now twist left, then right to score,
Ida Well's *Red Record* as Number Four!

Journalist Walter White infiltrated the Klan
and heard them brag about lynching—ah man!

One of them slapped his thigh—and declared it to be,
Quote; "The best show, Mister, I ever did see!"

The best show, Mister, I ever did see?!

"You ought to heard the wench howl when we strung her up!"
Heard the what, what? Go on, Shut up?!

(Loose position/break form.)

You're losing your balance—Mad I see!
Twist your behind back into position! *You serious?*
One, Two—Three!

(Move quickly back into position and continue the dance.)

Fifth Step—reach then ball into the blues,
Bessie Smith and W. C. Handy—the gut-bucket blues!

Sixth Step—stand upright in a glide
as you draw arms smoothly back to your sides.
Mary Bethune and Benjamin Mayes.
Educators, clearing the haze!

Seventh Step—Josephine no doubt
and Muhammad Ali, arms way out!

Last Step—palms on the desk. We talkin' Muse.
Zora Neale Hurston and Langston Hughes!

Slave ship!
Hands to the sky!
Run!
Now twist—don't die!

Ball into blues—
glide upright!
Arms triumphant!
Sho' you're right!

24

I Must Remember! (Song)

Sing this with your partner. (You sing the main lines and your partner sings the italicized words.)

I almost gave up—almost gave in—
almost forgot the distance we've been.
I almost let anger get the best of me.
I almost, almost couldn't see.

But when they bombed King's house
did he stop? *No.*
When they came against Malcolm,
did he flop? *No.*

When they locked up Rosa, knocked Harriet in the head,
did they give up their dreams, walk away instead?

I must remember—*draw strength from their love.*
I must remember—*draw strength from their courage.*
I must remember—*I must go on.*
I must remember—*I must be strong.*

Our ancestors were chained in the bottom of ships.
They were denied their freedom. They endured the whips.
They never gave up—never gave in.
Our ancestors danced freedom—and we must again!

I must remember—*remember*—draw strength from their love.
I must remember—*remember*—draw strength from their courage.
I must remember—*remember*—I must go on.
I must remember—*rememb*er—I must be strong.

25

Reinforcements: Voices of Wisdom

"Power concedes nothing without demand—it never has and never will."
Fredrick Douglass, abolitionist

"Now I done born thirteen children—and seen most all of them sold off to slavery, and when I cried out in my mother's grief, none but Jesus heard me."
Sojourner Truth, women's rights activist

"I hated every minute of training, but I said, 'Don't quit. Suffer now and live the rest of your life as a champion.'"
Muhammad Ali, boxer and Heavyweight Champion of the World

"Forgiveness is not an occasional act—it is a constant attitude."
Martin Luther King Jr., civil rights leader and visionary

"Remember who you are and whose you are."
Sister Thea Bowman, woman of God

26

The Spiritual Blueprint: The Great Procession

The dance of liberation isn't "Hands in the air" or "Assume the position". With Charles M. Blow's question, "At what precise pace should a black man walk to avoid suspicion?" and President Obama's acknowledgment of having been followed while shopping in stores, and Zimmerman's attorney's assertion that Trayvon had four minutes to run, it seems this dance of survival has become quite complicated.

What steps should you take in the face of oppression? How should you proceed toward adulthood? How do you dance in a way that honors your humanity and glorifies the God of love and justice? Certainly the words of the Dr. King during the Civil Rights Movement resonate: "A man can't ride your back unless it's bent!"

So do the words of the more contemporary Rev. T.D. Jakes: "We cannot become distracted. When things appear impossible and your situation challenging, keep your eyes on Jesus and keep moving forward!"

In light of this wisdom, look at these eight significant walks from Genesis to Revelation for a more ethical choreography.

Say this with your partner. (You say the italicized words.)

The Great Procession

Stand outside of Eden,
know God never leaves nor forsakes!

March around Jericho,
shout down the walls till they break!

Step into the ark,
not everybody's getting on the boat!

Trudge toward Egypt,
admit betrayal—mend the coat!

Stand before your Red Sea
and regardless of how you feel,
trust God to fight your battle
if you just keep still!

Journey toward Bethlehem,
follow the Shining way,
offer your best to the King;
discern the Herod's of the day!

Stand at Calvary,
as Jesus commends His Spirit with a nod.
Know your new life is unstoppable,
this truly is the Son of God!

Imagine yourself with the multitudes,
praising before the throne.
See clearly that His Word is light,
and you were never alone!

Review

Understand these words. Exercise new consciousness.

- ✓ Strategies
- ✓ Antislavery Movement
- ✓ Back-to-Africa Movement
- ✓ Ku Klux Klan
- ✓ The blues
- ✓ Courage
- ✓ Power
- ✓ Champion
- ✓ Red Sea
- ✓ Calvary

You learned that our New Ringshout Dance consists of eight strategic positions taken by ancestral couples that continue to inspire us today. You learned you can draw instruction on how to righteously conduct yourself in the world by looking in the Word of God, specifically at eight *walks* that enlightened men and women have taken in their procession toward God.

What important lesson that you learn while negotiating strategies?

____

Other positions have served us well. For instance, the crossed and linked arms during the Civil Rights marches allowed for support, cohesion and resistance among the demonstrators. Name another (other than the victory dance performed after an NBA championship game).

____

____

The Fourth Xenia Challenge

I

Interrogate!

Interrogate Self to Uncover Obstacles That Could Block Progress: The Symbolic Sacrifice

For I know the thoughts that I think towards you, says the Lord, thoughts of peace and not evil, to give you a future and a hope.

Jeremiah 29:11 (NKJV)

27

The Symbolic Sacrifice

For this fourth challenge, ask yourself, what could stop you on your journey. Anger could have stopped you earlier; other things still might. At the heart of the question is identifying the one thing that you are most afraid of.

The answer could be being embarrassed to the bone, having the fear of failure, or dying of humiliation in front of everybody.

But this, Young Initiate, is part of the purpose of a rite of passage. You will let go part of yourself today because you will see the greater part you can become. You can't hold on to the things of a child and call yourself a man, woman, or adult.

The Word of God in 1 Corinthians 13:11 (NKJV) reads: "When I was a child, I spoke as a child, I thought as a child, but when I became a man, I put childish things aside."

Rosa Parks, mother of the Civil Rights Movement, put it this way: "I have learned over the years that when one's mind is made up, this diminishes fear; knowing what must be done does away with fear."

28

A Serious Consideration: Young People Rule

Children, this is your world. Come out. Stand up! Earn it!

Maya Angelou

We are at war for the hearts, minds, and souls of our people and free-thinking people in the United States and throughout the world.

Haki Madhubuti

Some boys and girls in our history put aside childish things in a public and courageous manner. Their individual initiation into adulthood fueled our collective rite of passage as a nation. These young people were serious. When they left school, it wasn't to play hooky.

The Children of Alabama

Eight hundred students from Jefferson County, Alabama left their classrooms and assembled in groups of fifty. Knowing they could face abuse and imprisonment, they walked *five* miles to Birmingham to join the other marchers.

The Little Rock Nine

The Little Rock Nine of Arkansas, after the Supreme Court's Brown versus the Board of Education decision, moved toward the all-white school, passing through vicious hecklers kept at bay by the *ten* thousand National Guardsmen ordered in by President Ike Eisenhower.

The Wilmington Ten

The Wilmington Ten were accused, convicted, and sentenced to years of imprisonment. They sacrificed their innocence and held fast to their integrity. These young people were not street gangs, offended because somebody stepped on their "kicks". They confronted real and legal gangs, who would beat down your momma in front of you and take out one of their own for standing with you.

Think of one thing you're willing to let go of as a sign of your decision to attain manhood or womanhood. Do you have any such thing that could serve as sacrifice?

29

The Inquiry: Necessary Questions

Perform this with your partner! (Your partner says the first line and you follow with the italicized words, and so on.)

Suppose you were giving up weed?
Would I be making exceptions for that?
And what about joining gangs?
Would I justify that?

And cheating on your people?
Not being the best you can be?
Slipping, sliding, selling out?
Would I defend that, G?

Check the mirror!
Do I see respect?
Beyond flexing and sexing and all of that,
It's a man's soul, Son, that must stand erect!

Dawg? The "N" word?
Where's my pride?
I brought it to you straight.
I'm speaking as a guide.

When you become a man, Son,
you leave childish things aside!

Read it again, please.
I know that's twice.
Do you have any such thing
that could serve as sacrifice?

Yes, calling my boy the "N" word.
I let go of that—no doubt.

Well done, Young Initiate!
That's what I'm talking about.
When you're on a mission,
you stay en route!

Other sacrifices could include giving up the practice of self-sabotaging your success! Give up *dumbing down* your intelligence to fit in with others. Let go of performing below your capacity in response to those who expect and project failure.

Give up playing off your God-given gifts.

30

Your Symbolic Sacrifice: Write It Here

If you extend your soul to the hungry and satisfy the afflicted soul, then your light shall dawn in the darkness, and your darkness shall be as the noonday. The Lord will guide you continually, and satisfy your soul in drought, and strengthen your bones; You shall be like a watered garden, and like a spring of water, whose waters do not fail. Those from among you shall build the old waste places; You shall be called Repairer of the Breach, The Restorer of Streets to Dwell In.

Isaiah 58: 10-12 (NKJV)

Write your symbolic sacrifice vertically (up to God), and your goal five years from now horizontally (relating to fellow humanity and career). This will make the shape of a cross.

31

Determination: Check This Out

A married couple, Ellen and William Craft (after the Fugitive Slave Law of 1850 that provided for the return of slaves who escaped from one state into another) disguised themselves and escaped in a wagon—she as a white male planter, and he as her personal servant.

William "Box" Brown" escaped in Virginia by hiding himself inside an express package and sending the box as freight to Philadelphia, which was delivered to 107 North *Fifth* Street in Philadelphia, the offices of the Pennsylvania Antislavery Society.

Cut the excuses. Start preparing now. Do what you have to do to become who you are called to be.

32

The Crossing: Life Sacrifices

Bloody Sunday
On Bloody Sunday, March 7, 1965, six hundred marchers headed out of Selma, Alabama, to Montgomery. They were protesting for voting rights and against the death of Jimmie Lee Jackson, who had been murdered three weeks earlier after being beaten and then shot by a state trooper while trying to protect his mother during a demonstration. At the Edmund Pettus Bridge, police fired tear gas into the crowd and beat the marchers. Fifty were hospitalized.

Turnaround Tuesday
Four hundred fifty religious leaders, including Unitarian Universalist ministers Orloff Miller, James Reeb, and Clark Olsen, joined demonstrators for a second march over the bridge. That night, the three were attacked at a whites-only restaurant. Reeb's injuries were fatal.

March to Montgomery
On March 21, eight thousand assembled at Brown Chapel, including leaders of various races and religions. The march was limited to three hundred for two days. On March 24, they entered Montgomery County, and a Stars for Freedom rally was held with Harry Belafonte, Tony Bennett, Frankie Lane, Sammy Davis Jr., Nina Simone, and Peter, Paul, and Mary. The next day, 25,000 demonstrators joined the marchers at the state Capitol. That night, klansmen killed Viola Liuzzo, a Unitarian Universalist laywoman and mother of five.

The best way we can honor those who sacrificed for truth and freedom is to safeguard and expand it in the lives of others.

33

The Spiritual Blueprint: God's Sacrifice

Looking in the spiritual realm, we know what God gave. The Word of God tells us in John 3:16 (NKJV): "For God so loved the world that He gave His only begotten Son that whoever believes in Him would not perish but have everlasting life."

34

The Blood of Christ

I know it was the Blood.
I know it was the Blood.
I know it was the Blood for me!

One day when I was lost
My Savior died upon the cross.
And I know it was the Blood for me!

Spiritual

35

Ten Signs and Wonders: A Wonder-Working God

Lift ev'ry voice and sing, till earth and heaven ring! Ring with the harmonies of liberty!

Black National Anthem/James Weldon Johnson

Salvation is God's greatest miracle. It reconciles us with Our Creator and makes us Blood-bought children of Our Father. In His generosity, He continues to send signs, wonders, and miracles that give evidence of His love. These ten signs are truly amazing!

1. That we made it through the Middle Passage and are here today forty million strong.

2. That Harriet Tubman escaped slavery, returned nineteen times and freed more than three hundred people, dreamed variations of the escape routes, and was never captured, despite a $10,000 reward on her head.

3. That Crispus Attucks, a runaway slave, was the first American to shed blood in the revolution that freed America from British rule.

4. That President Abraham Lincoln went into a room and pleaded to God for victory in the Civil War at Gettysburg, and the nation's tide turned in a day.

5. That the fifth little girl who was bombed at 16th Street Baptist Church in Birmingham, did not die.

6. That the bomb at 16th Street Baptist Church that mortally injured the head of one of the children simultaneously (and solely) blew out the face of Christ in the stained-glass window.

7. That children from Wales halfway around the world replaced the window with the depiction of the risen Black Lord with

His outstretched arms, and the words, "Whatsoever you do to the least of my brethren that you do unto me."

8. That Martin Luther King Jr. didn't sneeze after a deranged woman stabbed him with the tip of the blade coming within a centimeter of his aorta, the main artery, and he lived to fulfill his mission.

9. That King's "I Have a Dream" speech at the 1963 March on Washington, (still to this day the largest demonstration for equality in the history of America, attended by 250,000 people) was delivered extemporaneously after his prepared speech when Mahalia Jackson shouted from the platform, "Tell them about the dream, Martin!"

10. That when the grave of Medgar Evers was opened thirty years after his martyrdom, his body was perfectly preserved. And his son was able, by the grace of God, to look at his father's face.

Hearing about this, some might say, "Folks back then sure had good embalmers!"

That may be so, but the indisputable truth is that we have a great God.
A God who says to the roaring sea, "go here and no further."
A God who will not let his anointed ones suffer corruption.
A God so powerful He raised Himself from the dead.

So gain, at the conclusion of this fourth Xenia challenge, what are you afraid of that our God can't handle?

Review

Make sure you are familiar with these very important terms.

- ✓ Hope
- ✓ Adult
- ✓ Civil Rights Movement
- ✓ Sacrifice
- ✓ Pride
- ✓ Tenacity
- ✓ Black National Anthem
- ✓ The March on Washington
- ✓ Martyr
- ✓ Courage

You learned that there is a part of you that you will let go of to symbolize the greater part you will become, and that that greater part is the life of Christ.

What is the most important lesson you learned while interrogating self to overcome obstacles?

____

____

Name another sign or wonder that you have witnessed in life.

____

You have presented your five-year goal. Give five steps you must take to achieve it.

____

____

____

____

The Fifth Xenia Challenge

A

Adapt!

Adapt Necessary Changes for Positive Adjustments in Self and Environment: Taking on the Other

By this all will know that you are my disciples, if you have love for one another.

John 13:35 (NKJV)

36

Immunizing against Hate: Taking on the Other

Carter G. Woodson, Father of African American history and founder of Black History Week (which later became Black History Month in February), says: "The bondage of the Negro brought captive from Africa is one of the greatest dramas in history, and the writer who merely sees in that ordeal something to approve or condemn fails to understand the evolution of the human race."

The first change you have to adapt to is that no one will be asking you anything.

Your challenge is to pose your own question like an adult and answer it!

There's one little hook. The question you pose must be related to the idea of Xenia—encountering or taking on *the other*. Xenia is about encountering the other in a *positive* way that allows each one to coexist and grow. It's providing hospitality and not being afraid to love. It's taking on a bit of the other to make you stronger. It's a kind of immunization against hate— a kind of communion.

And the spiritual mystery?

Putting on Christ, of course.

37

The Global Table: When We Encounter Other Cultures

Say this with your partner! (You say the italicized words.)

When our leaders sat at the global table, they knew their role.
They encountered other cultures. They X-rayed the soul
of red folk, and white folk, and yellow and brown.
They exalted the good wherever it was found!

And they sought out consciously without arrogance or shame
ideas that could bring life and ignite the flame!
King! Where did he get his idea for a bus boycott?
From Mahatma Gandhi! Correct! Am I not?

And Josephine's idea of adopting a rainbow tribe?
From the French who took her in when America wouldn't vibe!
And calling Harriet Tubman "Moses"? Do you know?
"From the prophet who told Pharaoh, "Let my people go!"

And it wasn't just one way. Good ideas just keep giving birth.
At that same table, we offered gifts of immeasurable worth.
Look at the man at Tiananmen Square, shouting before a tank,
"We shall overcome!" Take our words to the bank!

Look at Mandela drawing strength from us while incarcerated,
"Your freedom and mine cannot be separated."
And look again at Egypt's and Libya's young revolutionaries
holding signs that say, "By any means necessary!"

And the Chicano, women's, and Native American movements, too,
all of them revitalized by what we say and do!
Xenia! The global table where you take and give what you must,
and to complete your passage, pose your own question, we trust.

38

A Response: Young People, Speak

Say this response aloud!

Yes, Elders. We are ready
to show that we are able.

And our question is
What do we bring to this table?

The gift that I bear is: *(Write)* ______________________________

I bring something you cannot get
from a shelf.

I bring the wealth of my culture,
my God-given self.

Honest. Unapologetic.
Unafraid to share and to be

all that I am called
to be!

39

The Spiritual Blueprint: The Ultimate Transformation

And as they were eating, Jesus took bread, and blessed it, and broke it, and gave it to the disciples and said, 'Take, eat; this is My body;" then He took the cup, gave thanks, and gave it to them saying, "Drink from it, all of you. For this is My blood of the new covenant, which is shed for the remission of sins.

Matthew 26:26-28 (NKJV)

We know what Jesus brought to the global table. He brought the bread and wine. His Body and Blood! His Soul and Divinity! He brought His loving, saving self that we may live!

40

The Xenia Induction

In Matthew 5:14-16 (NKJV), the Word of God says: "You are the light of the world. A city that is set on a hill cannot be hidden. Nor do they light a lamp and put it under a basket, but on a lampstand, and it gives light to all who are in the house. Let your light so shine before men, that they may see your good works and glorify your Father in heaven."

41

The Xenia Pledge

Say aloud the Xenia Pledge.

I take the word, Xenia,
given at the start
and hold it as an emblem
upon my willing heart.

I'll continue to X-ray the soul
as a child of God indeed.
His Commandments and sacred wounds
are the gifts I truly need.

I'll continue to Exalt!
The name Jesus is above all names.
I will take it as my cover
and be safe in His flame.

I'll continue to Negotiate!
The greatest strategy I can employ
is to position myself rightly
in His approval and joy.

I'll continue to Interrogate!
I will not fear—I'll take the lead.
Our Lord has overcome the world.
I make that my abiding creed.

And I'll continue to Adapt!
I take His life as my own.
I'll be what I'm called to be—
in a word—*grown!*

42

Acknowledgment

Now our community
proudly acknowledges
the young man—
the young woman—in you.

Since you acknowledge the same,
boldly say and write: "I do!"

I do! (Write) ______________________________

43

The Ringshout Rap! (Finale)

Rap this with your partner! (You say the italicized words)

There ain't no contradiction—
just the pure-as-light conviction
that this life, it ain't no fiction,
Let it roll, See!
The living scroll's the key.

Martin and Malcolm
DuBois and Booker T.
The million plus the ten
coming strong with me!
Wonder-working soul
Majo, free!

Take what you need.
Grow and be true
Our legacy to the world
now challenges you.

Our legacy to the world
now challenges you.

44

Write The Vision: Make It Plain

Protect the young flock—until they have learned—
Give them respect beyond that which is earned.

Estella Conwill Majozo

The following is an open letter to parents, guardians, and the enlightened generation!

Now I will relate how Xenia came to be the guiding principle of this passage. As a parent of a young African American son, I came before our Creator and asked for the wisdom to bring him to godly manhood. In time, I fell asleep and found myself standing before three angels or ancestors in white who immunized my son. One of them handed me a torn-off piece of paper folded in quarters. I opened it and read the word, *Xenia,* written there. "Hey," I said as they who were leaving, "he's already had this one!" The middle one turned back and said before fading, "You never get too much of this one."

I didn't understand then the meaning of the word: "Being at home in your own cultural skin but not being afraid to let others in." I did not know that Xenia is a city in Ohio that was an important station on the Underground Railroad. I didn't know it was the location of Wilberforce University (the first college owned and operated by African Americans), and that it is, in fact, the geographical crossroads of this paradoxical promise land.

In time I came to know all this and more—namely that the worst super tornado recorded in the twentieth century had torn through the territory years before, stripping buildings from their foundations, taking lives, and sweeping some of our most treasured chronicles, memories, relics, and dreams from the university vaults and shelves into the screaming streets.

I came to understand that the torn-off piece of paper in a dream was possibly a remnant of our recurring rupture and a reminder of our need for renewal.

We must create a sense of wholeness together. We must create new rituals and truly become repairers of the breach. We must consciously reclaim our children. We must deliberately renew our minds—more than once—as a way of life!

I made Xenia first the guiding principle of my parenting, and then the basis for a new play entitled *Ringshout the Route*, which was produced at the Juneteenth Festival, and also as a college course at the University of Louisville and at Xavier University in New Orleans.

The original intention came full circle with *Ringshout: A National Rite of Passage*. It was an interactive initiation for teens that included workshops in leadership, history, music, dance, and cultural values, conducted by a brilliant team of teachers, facilitators, actors, and musicians committed to the survival, growth, and inspiration of this promised generation.

In this, its *fifth* manifestation, Ringshout is distilled from its many renderings, enhanced with the spirituality that undergirds the truth of our history, and offered as a manual for a national rite of passage.

I hope and pray that you will be inspired to nurture your own dreams, contribute to the empowerment of young people, and believe even more passionately in our amazing God who truly loves and sustains us.

45

Shine!

Shine like souls making light
in the bottom of ships.
Like spirituals rising sacred
from ancestors' lips.
Like wet ink signing
the great emancipation.
Like you truly see yourself
a new creation.

Shine like countless stars
in the sky of Abraham.
Shine like your ring has shouted
and it's your time to jam.
Shine like the face of Medgar
defying the grave.
Like kings and queens who will never
again be depraved.

Shine like you're giving glory,
glory, glory to the King.
Like you're graced by love
in every little thing.
Shine like you're honorable.
Shine with destiny.
Shine like you know your name.
Shine like you're free!

Review

Remember and take to heart these important terms.

- ✓ The Global Table
- ✓ Black History Month
- ✓ Montgomery Bus Boycott
- ✓ Culture
- ✓ Covenant
- ✓ Induction
- ✓ Creed
- ✓ Legacy
- ✓ Spirituals
- ✓ Destiny

You learned that you must now go forth into the world with a sense of purpose and self-possession. You must make your own Xenia pronouncements. As you bring your new life to the global table, remember there is no such thing as having too much grace. Act in hospitality. Exercise your humanity. And above all, love!

What is the most important lesson you learned with adapting necessary changes for positive adjustments in yourself and the world?

____

____

CERTIFICATION

CONGRATULATIONS!

You have successfully completed

RINGSHOUT!

A National Rite Of Passage

Your Name: (Signed)

____

Your Partner: (Signed)

____

DATE: _______________________________________

RINGSHOUT ELDERS (Signed)

Estella Conwill Majozo, PhD, and William L. Conwill, PhD

An Open Invitation To Life-Long Learning

When you're on a mission, you stay en route! *Ringshout! A National Rite of Passage* is an initiation, a beginning. Here are some cultural resources for further research that can aid in the process of your life-long learning.

You can find *ten* important references in each of the twenty categories that include a little important fact on the *five* or the *ten*. You can draw from thousands of other references. This compilation is simply a common starting point and an invitation for you as a culture-bearer and child of God to continue to grow and to be a positive, shining influence in the world.

1

Ten Classical Books You Should Know

1. *The Holy Bible*
2. *Souls of Black Folk* by W.E.B. DuBois
3. *Up From Slavery* by Booker T. Washington
4. *Why We Can't Wait* by Martin Luther King Jr.
5. *Autobiography of Malcolm X* by Alex Haley
6. *Narrative of the Life of Frederick Douglass: An American Slave* by Frederick Douglass
7. *I Know Why The Caged Bird Sings* by Maya Angelou
8. *Their Eyes Were Watching God* by Zora Neale Hurston
9. *A Raisin in the Sun* by Lorraine Hansberry
10. *From Slavery to Freedom* by John Hope Franklin and Evelyn Higginbotham

A little important fact: Did you know that the dramatic conflict in the award-winning play, *A Raisin in the Sun*, is sparked by a *ten*-thousand-dollar insurance check?

Write the title of your favorite book and explain why you like it.

____

____

2

Ten Classical Films You Should Know

1. *Roots: The Sage of An American Family*, written by Alex Haley
2. *Sankofa*, directed by Haile Gerima
3. *Daughters of the Dust*, directed by Julie Dash
4. *Boys in the Hood*, directed by John Singleton
5. *Malcolm X*, directed by Spike Lee
6. *Rosewood*, directed by John Singleton
7. *The Great Debaters*, directed by Denzel Washington
8. *Lilies of the Field*, starring Sidney Poitier
9. *Glory*, starring Denzel Washington and Morgan Freeman
10. *Coach Carter*, directed by Thomas Carter

A little important fact: Did you know that Alex Haley's research on the novel, *Roots: The Sage of An American Family,* which was later produced into a TV miniseries, took *ten* years, including visiting the village of Juffure where he listened to a griot tell the story of Kunta Kinte's capture?

Find your favorite film on YouTube or Netflix and fast forward to the scene you like best. Write why it excites you.

____

3

Ten Significant Cultural Songs You Should Know

1. "Lift Every Voice and Sing" (Black National Anthem)
2. "Strange Fruit" by Billie Holiday
3. "Four Women" by Nina Simone
4. "Oh Freedom" by Fisk Jubilee Singers
5. "Precious Lord, Take My Hand" by Thomas A. Dorsey
6. "Old Man River" by Paul Robeson
7. "Amazing Grace" by John Newton
8. "Respect" by Aretha Franklin
9. "Eye on the Sparrow" by Mahalia Jackson
10. "Say It Loud! I'm Black and I'm Proud!" by James Brown

A little important fact: Did you know that "Lift Every Voice and Sing" by James Weldon Johnson and his brother J. Rosamond Johnson was first performed by *five* hundred school children celebrating Lincoln's birthday?

Write the title of your favorite song. Write an inspirational line from the lyric below.

____

4

Ten Revolutionary Athletes You Should Know

1. Muhammad Ali
2. Olympic Three: Tommie Smith, John Carlos, Peter Norman
3. Bill Russell
4. Jessie Owens
5. Jackie Robinson
6. Paul Robeson
7. Wilma Rudolph
8. Joe Louis
9. Althea Gibson
10. Florence Griffith Joyner (Flo Jo)

A little important fact: Did you know that after Carlos and Smith raised their fists at the Olympics that *Time* magazine showed the *five*-ring Olympic logo with the words, "Angrier, Nastier, Uglier" instead of "Faster, Higher, Stronger"?

Write the name of your favorite athlete! Magic Johnson? Michael Jordan? Research and find one important fact about him or her that you did not know.

____

____

5

Ten Classical Speeches You Should Know

1. "What to the Slave is the Fourth of July?" by Frederick Douglass
2. Democratic National Convention Speech by Fanni Lou Hamer
3. Democratic National Convention Address by Jessie Jackson
4. "I've Been to the Mountaintop" by Martin Luther King Jr.
5. "The Sword and the Robe" by Thurgood Marshall
6. Inaugural Address 2009 by President Barack Obama
7. "Ain't I Woman?" by Sojourner Truth
8. "Atlanta Compromise" by Booker T. Washington
9. NAACP Speech Against Lynching by Ida B. Wells
10. "Message to the Grassroots" by Malcolm X

A little important fact: Did you know that Obama said this in a 2008 speech in Columbia, Missouri, just before the presidential election? "Now, Mizzou, I just have two words for you tonight: *Five* days....We are five days away from fundamentally transforming the United States of America."

Pick one speech from this list and listen to it on the Internet.

6

Ten National Organizations You Should Know

1. The National Association for the Advancement of Colored People (NAACP)
2. Universal Negro Improvement Association (UNIA)
3. National Urban League
4. National Urban Coalition
5. Southern Christian Leadership Conference (SCLC)
6. The United Negro College Fund
7. Rainbow Coalition
8. The Congressional Black Caucus
9. National Council of Negro Women
10. National Action Network

A little important fact: Did you know that the NAACP focused on *five* major areas from 1920 until 1950: anti-lynching legislation, voter participation, employment, due process under the law, and education?

Write the title of one organization at school or in your community that you belong to.

____

7

Ten Important Inventors and Scientists You Should Know

1. Benjamin Banneker
2. Charles Drew
3. Daniel Hale Williams
4. Emmett Chappelle
5. Ernest Everett Just
6. Garrett Morgan
7. George Washington Carver
8. Mae Jemison
9. Marie Maynard Daly
10. Patricia Bath

A little important fact: Did you know that George Washington commissioned George Ellicott and French engineer Pierre L'Enfant to plan the construction of the nation's capital on a *ten*-square-mile area of land, that Ellicott asked Benjamin Banneker to be his assistant, and when L'Enfant quit and took the drafts back home, Banneker reproduced the plans from memory within two days?

What could you invent now that could make your life or the life of your loved ones easier?

8

Ten Important Political Steps You Should Know

1. The Emancipation Proclamation
2. The 13th Amendment to the US Constitution
3. The 14th Amendment to the US Constitution
4. The 15th Amendment to the US Constitution
5. The 19th Amendment to the US Constitution
6. US Supreme Court Decision, *Powell v. Alabama*
7. US Supreme Court Decision, *Shelley v. Kraemer*
8. The Civil Rights Act of 1963
9. US Supreme Court Decision, *Brown v. Board of Education of Topeka*
10. The 1964 Civil Rights Act

A little important fact: Did you know that the Emancipation Proclamation was a *five*-page, handwritten document? Or did you know that the Civil Rights Act of 1963, the nation's benchmark civil rights legislation, prohibits discrimination on the basis of *five* categories: race, color, religion, sex, or national origin?

What political issue should you be more consciously aware of today? How can you address this issue?

9

Ten Recipients of the Congressional Medal of Honor

1. William Barnes
2. William Carney Jr.
3. Robert Augustus Sweener
4. Second Lieutenant Vernon Baker (US Army)
5. Edward A. Carter (US Army)
6. Charley L. Thomas (US Army)
7. George Watson (US Army)
8. James Anderson Jr. (Marine Corps)
9. Corporal Freddie Stowers (US Army)
10. First Lieutenant John R. Fox (US Army)

A little important fact: Did you know that twelve Civil War soldiers became the first African Americans to receive the Medal of Honor—and all were members of the *five* regiments of US Colored Troops?

Name two virtues that are celebrated through the Congressional Medal of Honor that you should develop more fully in your own life.

____

10

Ten Classical Visual Art Works You Should Know

1. *The Harp* by Augusta Savage
2. *The Train* by Romare Beardon
3. *Underground Railroad Series* by Jacob Lawrence
4. *The Banjo Lesson* by Henry Ossawa Tanner
5. *Mother and Child* by Elizabeth Catlett
6. *Aspects of Negro Life* by Aaron Douglas
7. *Portrait of President Franklin Roosevelt on the Dime* by Edmonia Lewis
8. *April 4, 1968* by Sam Gilliam
9. *Tar Beach* by Faith Ringgold
10. *Black Girl's Window* by Betye Saar

A little important fact: Did you know that *Arts Magazine* proclaimed that Romare Bearden's *The Train* was "one of the *ten* most important prints of our time"?

Select two works of art from this list and look them up. Print out the one you like best and frame it in your room.

11

Ten Dramatic Plays You Should Know

1. *A Raisin in the Sun by* Lorraine Hansberry
2. *Purlie Victorious* by Ossie Davis, Philip Rose, and Peter Udell
3. *Blues for Mister Charlie* by James Baldwin
4. *Fences* by August Wilson
5. *For Colored Girls Who Have Considered Suicide When the Rainbow Is Enough* by Ntosake Shange
6. *Black Nativity* by Langston Hughes
7. *The Mountaintop by* Katori Hall
8. *Top Dog/Underdog by* Suzan-Lori Parks
9. *Escape; or A Leap to Freedom* by William Wells Brown
10. *The Dutchman by* Amiri Baraka

A little important fact: On the *ten!* Did you know that playwright August Wilson completed a *ten*-play cycle that chronicled African American life in the twentieth century?

On YouTube, look up the song, "Mary, Did You Know?" which is featured in the production of *Black Nativity.* Write a response to what you see.

____

12

Ten Classical Musicians/Composers You Should Know

1. Duke Ellington—"Take the 'A' Train"
2. Miles Davis—"Kind of Blue"
3. Louis Armstrong—"What a Wonderful World"
4. Charlie Parker—"Ornithology"
5. John Coltrane—"Giant Steps"
6. WC Handy—"St. Louis Blues"
7. Stevie Wonder—"Happy Birthday to You"
8. Margaret Bonds—"He's Got the Whole World in His Hands"
9. Scott Joplin—"Maple Leaf Rag"
10. Eubie Blake—"I'm Just Wild About Harry"

A little important fact: Did you know that Duke Ellington is one of only *five* jazz musicians ever to have been featured on the cover of *Time*?

Write the name of your favorite musician. Find out who influenced him or her.

____

13

Ten Classical Black Dance Companies You Should Know

1. Katherine Dunham Company
2. Alvin Ailey American Dance Theatre
3. Arthur Mitchell Dance Theatre of Harlem
4. Bill T. Jones/Arnie Zane Dance Company
5. Urban Bush Women
6. Lula Washington Dance Theatre
7. Philadanco
8. Ronald K. Brown's Evidence
9. Dallas Black Dance Theatre
10. The McIntosh County Shouters

A little important fact: Did you know that The McIntosh County Shouters is a *ten*-member Ringshout Gullah-Geechee group that began performing professionally in 1980?

Find out when the Alvin Ailey American Dance Theatre is coming to your city, save your money, buy the tickets, and go see them dance.

14

Ten Classical Comedians You Should Know

1. Bert Williams
2. Redd Foxx
3. Bill Cosby
4. Flip Wilson
5. Richard Pryor
6. Dick Gregory
7. Eddie Murphy
8. Moms Mably
9. Whoopi Goldberg
10. Martin Lawrence

A little important fact: Did you know that Dick Gregory and his wife raised *ten* children?

Write the name of your favorite comedian and tell why you like him or her.

____

15

Ten Entrepreneurs You Should Know

1. William Leidesdorff
2. James Forten
3. John H. Johnson
4. Bill and Camille Cosby
5. Oprah Winfrey
6. Madam C. J. Walker
7. Robert Johnson
8. Annie Malone
9. Arthur G. Gaston
10. Booker T. Washington

A little important fact: Did you know that Oprah Winfrey gave two five million-dollar gifts to Morehouse College?

What would your small business be if you were to establish one?

____

16

Ten Important Historians You Should Know

1. Carter G. Woodson
2. Dr. Yosef Ben-Jochannan
3. John Henrik Clarke
4. Dr. Ivan Van Sertima
5. Dr. Chancellor Williams
6. John Hope Franklin
7. C.L.R. James
8. Dr. Vincent Harding
9. Drusilla Dunjee Houston
10. Anna Julia Cooper

A little important fact: Did you know that Dr. Carter G. Woodson published *five* textbooks, *five* edited collections of documents, and *five* sociological studies?

Write a brief *five*-line history about your ancestry after asking a relative to give you five facts about your family that you did not know.

____

____

____

____

17

Ten Important Mirroring Warriors You Should Know

1. Toussaint Louverture
2. Olaudah Equiano
3. Kwame Nkrumah
4. Yaa Asantawaa
5. Patrice Lumumba
6. Nelson Mandela
7. Marcus Garvey
8. Ellen Johnson Sirlief
9. Mamphela Ramphele
10. William Wilberforce

A little important fact: Did you know that the Garvey Nationalist Movement was the greatest international movement of African peoples in modern times with more than eight million followers, and the youngest cadres were taken in at *five* years of age and then graduated to sections for older children?

Did you know that Nelson Mandela served *five* years as the first president of the new South Africa? Did you know that he joined the ancestors on December 5, 2013, and that his memorial in South Africa lasted *ten* days?

Name someone you know in this generation who crossed the color, class, or gender line to fight for Xenia equality and love.

____

18

Ten Important Lawyers You Should Know

1. William T. Green
2. Charles Hamilton Houston
3. Supreme Court Justice Thurgood Marshall
4. Samuel R. Lowery
5. Marion Wright Edelman
6. J. Alexander Chiles
7. Richard Theodore Greener
8. Benjamin Hooks
9. Johnnie Cochran
10. First Lady Michelle Obama

A little important fact: Did you know that First Lady Michelle Obama's *Let's Move!* Initiative has *five* pillars? 1) Creating a healthy start for children; 2) Empowering parents and caregivers; 3) Providing healthy food in schools; 4) Improving access to healthy, affordable foods; 5) Increasing physical activity.

What do you think about the lawyer commercials on television? What do these commercials reveal about the lawyer's place in society?

____

____

19

Ten Important Preachers and Their Sermons You Should Know

1. Reverend William J. Seymour—"Sacrificed on the Cross"
2. Reverend C. L. Franklin—"Dry Bones in the Valley"
3. Dr. Martin Luther King Jr.—"I've Been to the Mountaintop"
4. Reverend T.D. Jakes—"He-motions"
5. Reverend Noel Jones—"This One's on God"
6. Reverend Fred Shuttlesworth—Civil Rights Preacher
7. Reverend Creflo Dollar—"Change You Way of Thinking"
8. Reverend Juanita Bynum—"The Threshing Floor"
9. Reverend Father Giles A. Conwill—in "Under God a New Birth of Freedom" (award-winning bicentennial sermons)
10. Reverend Cindy Trimm—"I Know Who I Am"

A little important fact: Did you know that Rev. T.D. Jakes in 1996 moved his family and fifty other families from West Virginia to establish The Potter's House in Dallas, and as many as *five* thousand people attend each of the four three-hour services every weekend?

What is the most profound message you have ever heard from a minister of God?

____

____

____

20

Ten Remarkable Treasures You Should Know

1. "Lift Every Voice and Sing"
2. The Liberation Flag
3. The American Flag
4. Kwanzaa
5. Celebration of Black History Month
6. Howard University and all other HBCUs
7. The 16th Street Baptist Church and other churches upholding the values
8. Smithsonian National Museum of African American History and Culture, to open on the National Mall 2015
9. The Martin Luther King Jr. Monument in Washington, DC
10. The White House: The National Capitol of the United States of America

A little important fact: Did you know there are 105 historically Black Colleges and Universities (HBCU) in the United States?

An Amazing and Transformative Gift Book!

Estella Conwill Majozo combines her poetic voice, cultural knowledge, and prophetic vision to create *Ringshout! A National Rite of Passage.* Having evolved over the past fifteen years from a personal parenting primer to a dramatic work to a college course, *Ringshout* is now published as a resource guide, a gift for the new and promised generation. Sharing a deep personal and spiritual revelation, Majozo crafts five challenges around the word Xenia. These challenges engage the young participants in rich historical and cultural content through an interactive, creative, and communal experience.

***Ringshout* is a cultural call to action for the twenty-first century. Firmly rooted in the African American experience, it opens the door to participation across racial and ethnic lines. "Being at home in your own cultural skin but not being afraid to let other in." It is my vision and hope that *Ringshout* will become the model for best practices for youth development programs across the country.**

Priscilla Hancock Cooper
Interim President and CEO
Birmingham Civil Rights Institute

Ringshout! A National Rite of Passage is a tale of our great and powerful people who were called by Almighty God to survive the horrors of slavery and to resist some of the most brutal oppression inflicted upon mankind in the past five hundred years. It is an ongoing, interactive tale that functions as a rite of passage and features you, a member of the new and promised generation, as the main character—and as you step into your sacred purpose, an indomitable hero! Across race, ethnicity, class, and gender, you are invited to make this rite of passage and become a more enlightened, compassionate, mature, and spiritually empowered human being!

This is *your* Rite of Passage!
It is the truth about your past
and the key to your future.
You will grow and be blessed just by reading it.
It will change your life forever!

Made in the USA
Monee, IL
30 August 2022

12819324R00069